The Hanukkah Ghosts

MALKA PENN, author of *The Miracle of the Potato Latkes*, has also written articles, stories, and recipes for a number of magazines, including *Shofar, Young Judean*, and *World Over*. The mother of two grown children, she and her husband live in Storrs, Connecticut.

The Hanukkah Ghosts

Malka Penn

AN AVON CAMELOT BOOK

AVON BOOKS
A division of
The Hearst Corporation
1350 Avenue of the Americas
New York, New York 10019

Copyright © 1995 by Michele Palmer
Published by arrangement with Holiday House, Inc.
Visit our website at http://AvonBooks.com
Library of Congress Catalog Card Number: 94-15257
ISBN: 0-380-72838-9
RL: 3.9

First Avon Camelot Printing: December 1997

CAMELOT TRADEMARK REG. U.S. PAT. OFF. AND IN OTHER COUNTRIES, MARCA REGISTRADA,
HECHO EN U.S.A.

Printed in the U.S.A.

OPM 10 9 8 7 6 5 4 3 2 1

CHAPTER

I

A December dusk settled on the moor, turning it still and gray, like an old, faded photograph.

Susan shivered at the bleak Yorkshire landscape that stretched before her like an endless sea. Standing on a rock ledge overlooking the moor, she felt more than just an ocean away from her home in Connecticut. She felt she was at the very edge of the world.

As she zipped her jacket up to her chin, she recalled her great-aunt Elizabeth's warning:

"Don't go wandering the moor on your own, dear. You could easily get lost."

The girl didn't need advice from her great-aunt to keep from venturing onto that desolate terrain. Shivering again, she climbed down the ledge and hurried back toward Wimsley Hall.

With its stone gables and chimneys traced against a darkening sky, the manor house was almost as foreboding as the moor, but at least Aunt Elizabeth had promised that hot tea and a warm fire would be waiting for her.

As Susan approached the house, she scanned the rows of lead-latticed windows, half-expecting to see her great-aunt's face at one of them. Ever since the girl had arrived at the estate a few hours earlier, the old woman had been staring at her. That's why Susan had fled outside in the first place, mumbling something about fresh air's being a remedy for jet lag.

Standing in the gravel courtyard behind the house, she had the feeling she was still being watched. She hesitated, not ready to go in and be confronted by Aunt Elizabeth's gaze yet not wanting to remain alone outside, either.

A scratching noise in the distance attracted

her attention. Following the sound, she walked past empty stables toward the long oak-lined driveway. At the end of the driveway, just inside the black iron gate, she saw a figure in the shadows raking leaves.

She remembered her great-aunt's second warning—about the possibility of running into Ben, the old gardener.

"He means well, but he's rather gruff, I'm afraid. He's been here so long, he thinks he owns the place" was the way Aunt Elizabeth described him.

Susan didn't want to meet a gruff old man any more than she had wanted to wander out onto a desolate moor. Abruptly, she turned to go, but as she did, she tripped over a rock and stumbled into a thick layer of leaves.

"Can't you see those leaves are in a pile? Don't be scattering them about!" a voice from the shadows shouted at her.

"I'm sorry," she called back.

The gardener didn't respond, and Susan decided he must be deaf as well as grouchy. Cautiously, she made her way down the driveway, trying to avoid anything that resembled a pile of leaves.

When she was within a few yards of him, she repeated her apology in a loud voice.

"I said I'm sorry about the leaves."

He spun around, his rake in midair. Then, slowly, he lowered the rake and swiped the cap off his head.

"Beg your pardon, miss," he said. "I thought you might've been Alex up to no good."

He stared at her with an expression of curiosity not unlike Aunt Elizabeth's.

Susan returned his stare with one of equal curiosity. Instead of the old man she had expected, she was facing a boy, just slightly older than herself, fourteen or fifteen at the very most. Despite a chill in the air, he was wearing only a thin shirt and overalls.

"I guess I thought you were someone else, too," she said.

He stared at her a moment longer before he turned back to his raking.

"Getting dark," he muttered over his shoulder. "You'd best be inside."

A bell tinkled in the distance. Someone, probably Mrs. Spruce, Aunt Elizabeth's housekeeper, appeared in the front doorway of Wimsley Hall. She looked tiny and doll-like, framed by the light behind her.

"There you go," the boy said. "It's your teatime. They'll be waiting for you."

Then he struck a match and placed it in a pile of leaves. They crackled as they caught fire, filling the air with a pungent smell. He seemed hypnotized by the fire and didn't respond when Susan said good-bye and started up the driveway.

By the time the girl reached the front door, it was nearly dark. The only light in the front of the house came from two flickering candles in a second-story window and a golden sliver where Mrs. Spruce had left the door slightly ajar for her.

Before she went in, Susan glanced back toward the gate, but all she could see was a faint glow from the smoldering fire.

CHAPTER

2

"Do come in, dear. Mrs. Spruce has fixed a lovely tea."

Aunt Elizabeth was seated in a tall wing chair next to the fireplace in the library.

Susan entered the large wood-paneled room, made somewhat cozy by a blazing fire and several lamps casting small pools of warm light on the tables and walls.

Books were everywhere: dusty leatherbound volumes lined the shelves, and glossy new ones were scattered in piles on chairs, tables, even the floor. Next to Aunt Elizabeth, on top of a stack of books resting on the table, was a small, delicately carved brass menorah holding two unlit candles.

The girl took a seat opposite her great-aunt, waiting for the old woman to begin staring at her again. For now, though, Aunt Elizabeth was occupied with the details of the tea tray in front of her. It contained not just tea but cucumber sandwiches, baked beans, and a chocolate cake glazed with white icing.

She poured a cup of steaming tea and handed it to Susan.

"Milk and sugar?" she asked.

Susan shook her head—and immediately wished she hadn't. At the first sip, the hot liquid burned her tongue. Then some of it spilled into her lap as she hastily set the cup down.

Aunt Elizabeth didn't seem to notice. "Did the fresh air help your jet lag?" she inquired.

"I guess so," Susan said, trying to blot up the spill with her napkin. She reached for a cucumber sandwich to cool her burned tongue.

"I didn't go on the moor," she added. "I didn't feel like it."

She wanted her great-aunt to know that had

she wanted to, she would have done so, despite the warning.

The old woman looked at the girl over the teapot she was holding.

"I came here as a young bride more than fifty years ago," she said. "I couldn't bear the moor and its vastness then, either. I was very homesick, leaving London. Quite as much as you are now for Connecticut."

Susan blushed. "I'm not homesick. I'm used to being away from home. My father's always going on business trips and sending me somewhere."

"Well, I'm glad he decided to send you to Wimsley Hall for a week, although I wish he could have come with you. I would like to have seen him as well."

"He's very busy," Susan said.

"Yes, I suspect so."

Aunt Elizabeth picked up a small green leatherbound album and began flipping through the pages.

"That's him. That's your father," she said, pointing to a faded snapshot of a baby in the arms of a young woman.

Susan looked at the picture. It was hard to imagine her father that young.

"London was being bombed then. It was during World War Two, you know, and many children, including your father, were sent out of the city to the countryside. My brother and his wife—your grandparents—asked me to take him in, and I agreed. My husband was in the army, and I was very lonely. I took in another child as well—a Jewish refugee from Hitler's Europe."

Susan looked closely at the young woman holding the baby.

"Is that you?" she asked.

"Yes, that's me. That was taken shortly after he arrived."

She put the album down and picked up the menorah.

"It was at this very time of year, the first night of Hanukkah. I remember it because the other child had just lit her menorah."

She paused, as if picturing the scene.

"She gave the menorah to me when she left. I light it every Hanukkah and think about her and your father."

She paused again. "Did you know that to-night's the first night of Hanukkah?"

Susan shrugged. She didn't know. Why should she? She wasn't Jewish—at least she didn't think of herself that way. Her mother had been Jewish, but she died when Susan was very young, and her father didn't practice any religion in particular.

"Shall we light the Hanukkah candles?" Aunt Elizabeth asked.

Susan shrugged again. It seemed odd that her great-aunt, who wasn't Jewish either, would want to light Hanukkah candles, but if she wanted to light them, she should go ahead. Susan didn't care one way or the other.

"This is the shamash, the servant candle, as it was explained to me," Aunt Elizabeth said, pointing to the highest candle on the meno-rah. "We light it first, then use it to light a new candle for each night of Hanukkah."

She struck a match and lit the shamash. "There is a prayer, of course, for lighting the candles, but I must admit I've forgotten the exact words. It's something about thanking God for helping the Jewish people."

Susan wondered what the help was, but she didn't ask. Hesitantly, she took the shamash from her great-aunt and lit the other candle. After she replaced the shamash in its holder, she settled back in her chair.

For the first time since she had arrived at Wimsley Hall, she took a deep breath. The menorah candles were comforting. They seemed to warm her even more than the blazing fire in the fireplace.

For a brief moment, Susan had the strange sensation of déjà vu—the feeling that she was reliving something that had happened in exactly the same way before.

She tried to remember if she had ever lit Hanukkah candles. Maybe, she thought. Maybe when she was very little, when her mother was still alive.

Aunt Elizabeth cut a slice of cake and put it on Susan's plate.

"Tomorrow, right before breakfast, we'll have a walk-about on the moor," she said. "It's a good idea to get used to it."

Susan took a bite of the cake. "How did you get used to it?"

"Ah, that's a good question," her great-aunt said. "As a matter of fact, I avoided it for a very long time. I never went out on it. It seemed too vast, too lonely, and I was lonely enough.

"But one day, after my husband left for the war, and before your father arrived, I was inside, moping about as usual, I suppose, when Ben came rushing in.

" 'There's been an accident,' he said. 'Master Alex's been riding on the moor and he's fallen off his horse.' "

"Alex?" Susan sat up in her chair. That was the same name the boy raking leaves had mentioned.

"Alex was my husband's son by a previous marriage. His mother died shortly after he was born." Aunt Elizabeth stared at Susan. "Something like your situation."

Susan remained silent, her expression vacant. She didn't like to talk about her mother—least of all with strangers, even if they were relatives.

Aunt Elizabeth cleared her throat and continued. "Anyway, at that time Alex was about fifteen or so. When the accident happened, there was nothing I could do then to avoid the moor. I rang up the doctor in the village and went with him in his jeep to bring Alex back. Riding out there, worried about Alex, I somehow forgot about myself and lost my fear of the moor. After that, I went out there every day— and still do."

"What happened to Alex?" Susan asked, trying to sound casual.

"He broke his leg, quite badly, and needed crutches for a long time after that. He was always a difficult lad, and I'm afraid his accident only made him more difficult."

Susan wanted to tell her great-aunt about the boy she had seen raking and how he had mentioned someone named Alex, but she hesitated. Aunt Elizabeth might think she was making it up. Besides, she thought, it couldn't be the same Alex. Could it?

"Does he still live here?" Susan asked. "Alex, I mean?"

Aunt Elizabeth stared at her again for a moment before her face relaxed into a smile.

"Mrs. Spruce and I are the only residents of Wimsley Hall. And now, of course, you, for a week. But it's getting late and you must be quite tired after your trip."

Susan didn't need much persuasion to go upstairs to her room. As she undressed and settled into bed, she listened to the wind blowing off the moor. She thought about Alex and the Jewish refugee and her father as a baby, but mostly she thought about the boy she had seen raking leaves. Just before she fell asleep, she realized that she hadn't told him her name or asked him his.

CHAPTER

3

When Susan woke up the next morning, she looked around the unfamiliar room and pulled the covers back over her head. Any warmth she had felt in the glow of the Hanukkah candles the previous night had vanished in the gray light of morning.

The prospect of going out on the moor with her great-aunt seemed very disagreeable to her. She decided she would not go, even if Aunt Elizabeth begged and pleaded. She would not get out of bed or go down to breakfast until she was good and ready. She would not talk to anyone if she didn't feel like it. She would not—

A knock at the door ended her list of would-nots.

"I have a message from your aunt," Mrs. Spruce said, bustling into the room.

At first, Susan pretended to be asleep, but curiosity overcame her stubbornness and she pulled the covers down.

"What's the message?" she asked.

"She won't be taking you out on the moor this morning."

"Why not?" Susan sat up, surprised at her feeling of disappointment.

"She's had to go into the village," Mrs. Spruce said. "Ben is threatening to quit if she doesn't find someone to help with the raking. So she's gone into town to find a lad. She said she won't be back until she does."

Abruptly, Susan blurted out, "I saw a boy here yesterday who was raking."

"Did you now?" Mrs. Spruce said, looking at her with a suspicious sideways glance. "Well, he must have quit. They usually do. Ben's not an easy one to work for. Always grumbling, he is. Anyway, your aunt's gone for the morning."

"What will I do then?" Susan asked.

"She said you could rummage through the library. There're lots of books to read." Mrs. Spruce turned to go. "I'd like to stay and chat, but I've got work to do myself. Ben's not the only one around here who could use some help."

She left, closing the door behind her.

Susan threw off the covers and stomped over to her still-packed suitcase on the floor. She hadn't come all the way to England to sit in the house and read books, she told herself. She emptied the suitcase on the floor and sifted through her clothes for something to wear.

She was determined to go outside and find the boy and ask him his name and ask him about Alex. She didn't care what Mrs. Spruce said. She knew he was still around.

When she got dressed and came downstairs, Mrs. Spruce was in the kitchen, stirring the contents of various pots and pans.

"Your aunt said to remind you not to wander the moor by yourself," she called after the girl, who had grabbed a muffin and was heading out the door.

"I'm not going on the moor. I'm taking a walk around the house."

Outside, the air felt fresh, almost springlike, not at all like a December day. The sun had burned through early morning fog, leaving only a sheer, shimmering mist above the trees.

Susan walked down the driveway to the gate, past several large mounds of leaves. She saw the ashes from the pile of leaves the boy had burned yesterday. But she didn't see him or hear his raking; she didn't see or hear anyone, for that matter.

Disappointed, she walked up the driveway slowly, past the empty stables to the back of the estate, and found herself on the same rock ledge where she had stood yesterday.

The moor looked much more inviting in the morning sunshine than it had at dusk. In fact, the boundless open space that had made her turn away from it before now made her feel adventurous. Breathing in the fresh, sweet-smelling air, she thought she'd been silly for being afraid yesterday.

She stepped off the ledge and started down

the slight incline that marked the edge of the moor. Her destination was a pile of rocks about a hundred yards ahead of her. She wouldn't go any farther than that, she decided—not unless she wanted to.

All around her, as far as she could see, a low-growing purplish-brown plant covered the ground. She stooped down to pinch off a sprig of it. The tiny sprig comforted her, much as the candles had the night before, and she held it in her hand as she strode toward the rock pile.

Every once in a while she looked behind her to make sure the house was still in sight. Even when a small ridge in the landscape caused it to disappear, she kept going anyway. She was certain she would see it from the rocks, which were just a few yards ahead of her now.

But when she got to the rock pile, the house was still hidden from view. She turned all around. There were ridges everywhere.

She started running off in one direction, and then another. Every way she tried, all she could see was the moor.

When she began scrambling up still another ridge, a large reddish-brown bird jumped out of the scrubby bushes directly in front of her. It was flapping its wings and chattering something that sounded like "Go-back! Go-back! Go-back!"

She stopped, startled by the bird, but even more startled by the human voice behind her.

"He's right, you know. You could get lost around here without a guide."

Susan swirled around. Her great-aunt was standing on the opposite ridge, smiling and waving a picnic basket.

"I thought we could tramp about and have lunch over there," Aunt Elizabeth called out, pointing to a distant hill.

Susan was relieved to see her great-aunt, although, of course, she wouldn't admit it. She was also glad that Aunt Elizabeth wasn't angry at her for disobeying her warning.

As they set off toward the distant hill, she had to walk quickly to keep up with the old woman. Along the way, Aunt Elizabeth showed Susan paths and landmarks that would keep her from getting lost in the future. She also identified the bird as a red grouse and the plant as heather.

"It's important to know the names of plants and animals," she said, "as well as their habits. We can learn a lot just by observing them.

"Take the red grouse, for instance. He's the hardy type. He never flies south when it gets cold. He sticks it out right here on the moor, feeding on the heather all winter long.

"And the heather keeps right on going, too. It survives the wind and the cold and even the snow. It doesn't flower until August or September, but when it does, it's the prettiest thing you've ever seen."

She looked at Susan pointedly. "Some people are like that, too. They're late bloomers— but when they do bloom, they're quite exceptional."

After an hour of Aunt Elizabeth's natural history lessons, they reached the top of the hill. The valley on the other side looked like a giant patchwork quilt, with hedgerows and rock fences dividing the fields.

Aunt Elizabeth took a blanket from the basket and spread it on the ground. They ate their lunch watching a flock of sheep grazing in the distance. The old woman seemed not to stare at Susan so much, and the girl began to relax in her great-aunt's company.

It wasn't until the end of the day, when they were on their way back to Wimsley Hall, that she remembered the old woman's morning errand.

"Did you find someone to help Ben?" she asked.

"I'm afraid not," Aunt Elizabeth answered. "There's a shortage of young people willing to do that kind of work nowadays. At least Ben knows I tried, and hopefully that will satisfy him for a while."

The afternoon light was fading by the time they returned to Wimsley Hall. It was the same time of day when Susan had seen the boy yesterday. Maybe he was still hanging around, she thought. Maybe she could find him and convince him to stay on. It would certainly be a surprise for Aunt Elizabeth.

"I think I lost something down by the gate," she told her great-aunt. "I'll be in soon."

She walked along the driveway, past the empty stables, scanning the shadows for a glimpse of the boy. She paced back and forth twice by the iron fence that bordered the road. Reluctantly, she admitted to herself that Mrs. Spruce was right after all. The boy must have quit and wasn't coming back.

She was about to go inside when she heard a noise coming from the stables. It sounded like a horse neighing. Then she heard another sound from the same direction—that of human voices arguing.

She crept over to the front of the stables and looked through a dusty window into the dimly lit building. A bare light bulb hung from the ceiling, revealing two figures. One was the boy she had seen raking yesterday. The other was a boy about the same age, leaning on one crutch and wildly swinging another one in the air.

"You deliberately mis-shod the horse. You wanted him to throw me!" the boy with crutches screamed.

"Do you think I would risk the safety of a horse over the likes of you, Alex?" the other one screamed back.

"I'm Master Alex to you, Jamie!" He lunged forward with his crutch, but Jamie jumped out of the way, and Alex fell on the ground.

"You'll pay for this!" Alex cried. "You'll pay!"

A horse reared up in one of the stalls.

"Look what you're doing. You're scaring the animals."

Jamie stroked the horse in an attempt to calm him, then backed away toward the door.

"You can run away if you like," Alex shouted after him, "but she'll fire you when I tell her what you did! You'll see."

Susan held her breath as Jamie walked past her out of the stable. She was crouched behind the door now, but he didn't notice her. He just kept on walking down the driveway and out the gate.

Meanwhile, Alex picked himself up and hobbled a few steps outside on his crutches.

"She'll fire you! You'll see!" he shouted after

Jamie. Muttering to himself, he turned and disappeared into the woods.

Susan waited a few minutes before she came out of hiding, still shaken by the scene she had just witnessed. It wasn't only the argument and Alex's anger that upset her.

She thought about the story Aunt Elizabeth had told her of her stepson Alex, who had been crippled by a fall from a horse. Could this be the same Alex? she wondered. But how could it be? The accident had happened over fifty years ago.

Susan grew even more agitated when she thought about the horses. Where did they come from? The stables had been empty just minutes before.

She ran toward the house, so preoccupied with her thoughts that she didn't even see the three candles flickering in the upstairs window.

CHAPTER

4

"I was beginning to wonder if you were coming in for tea," Aunt Elizabeth said as Susan entered the library. "Did you find what you were looking for?"

The girl sat across from her great-aunt. She wanted to tell her about what she had just witnessed, but she was afraid again that she wouldn't be believed.

"I'm not sure," she said. "I mean, I found something."

She took the cup of tea Aunt Elizabeth handed her and gently set it down to cool.

"Are there still horses here?" she asked.

She wanted to sound casual, but she knew it didn't come out that way.

Aunt Elizabeth stared at her. "Why do you want to know?"

"I was just wondering."

"My husband had horses, but we sold them after the war."

"So the stables are empty?"

"Yes, except for some garden tools."

Susan took a sip of tea, trying to swallow it and her great-aunt's statement at the same time. Had she just imagined the horses and Alex and Jamie?

"I used to ride the horses into the village," Aunt Elizabeth continued. "There was a makeshift army hospital there during the war and I helped out, making beds and rolling bandages."

For a moment, Susan was distracted by the image of her great-aunt riding a horse.

"You rode a horse—instead of driving your car?"

"Petrol—that's gasoline to you—was rationed then. It was needed for the war."

"Who took care of my father when you were in the village?"

Aunt Elizabeth smiled. "Hanni did."

"Hanni? Was she the one who gave you the menorah?"

"You're full of questions tonight, aren't you? Yes, she gave me the menorah, and we should light it before we forget."

Aunt Elizabeth lit the shamash candle and handed it to Susan, who took it and lit the remaining two candles. Their light seemed to brighten the room even more than the lamps or the fire, and Susan watched their tiny dancing flames with fascination.

Aunt Elizabeth opened the photo album and placed it in Susan's lap. "That's Hanni," she said.

Susan looked at a picture of a solemn young girl about her age, her dark hair parted into two braids.

"There's a strong resemblance, don't you think?" Aunt Elizabeth asked.

"Resemblance?"

"Yes. Except for the braids, I think she looks a lot like you."

"I don't think so," Susan said, handing the album back to Aunt Elizabeth.

"Well, there's something about her that reminds me of you," Aunt Elizabeth said.

"She looks sad. I'm not sad. I told you yesterday that I don't get homesick."

"Yes, so you did. Well, she was certainly homesick. She had to leave her home in Vienna."

"Why?" Susan asked.

"Hitler was preaching hate, telling lies about the Jews, rounding them up and sending them to death camps, where they were murdered. She was one of the lucky ones who escaped."

Susan's eyes widened. She had learned about the Holocaust in school, but it hadn't seemed real to her until now.

Aunt Elizabeth looked at Susan's empty plate. "Aren't you going to have anything to eat?"

"I'm not hungry, and I'm very tired. I think I still have jet lag."

"The moor air can make one tired, too. You'll feel better after a good night's sleep."

That night, Susan lay in bed listening to the

sound of the wind crying. She thought about the scene in the stables and about Jews being sent to death camps.

It took her a long time to fall asleep, and when she finally did, she dreamed about getting lost on the moor, then looking into a mirror and seeing Hanni's face staring back at her.

CHAPTER

5

In the morning light, the incident at the stables seemed like a dream to Susan. She decided she must have imagined it after all. Besides, Aunt Elizabeth had confirmed that the stables were empty and that there hadn't been horses there for years. Still, the argument between Jamie and Alex had been so vivid that Susan felt compelled to go back and make sure.

After breakfast she walked over to the stables, but even before she went inside, she knew what she would find. Nothing.

The outside of the building had the look and feel of a place long deserted. When she lifted the rusty latch and swung open the door, she stepped inside an empty building. She peered into every stall. Not only were there no horses, but there was no water in the troughs, no smell of fresh hay or manure.

Susan walked back and forth over the dirt floor, as if by doing so she could somehow conjure up the people and horses and events she had seen—or thought she had seen—yesterday. All she felt, though, was more confusion than ever.

Were the horses she had seen ghosts? she wondered. Was Jamie a ghost? Was Alex? Alex was certainly frightening, but not because he seemed to be ghostlike in any way. If anything, he was more real than Susan cared him to be. But if he was so real before, where was he now?

"Who's messing around in there?"

Susan jumped at the sudden appearance of a slightly stooped old man who stepped out of the shadows.

"I—I'm not messing around," she stuttered.

"Well, what are you doing in here?" he snarled.

"I'm just looking."

"There's nothing to see. Hasn't been anything for a long time." He glanced about. "You seen a rake around here?"

Susan looked behind her and spied one propped against a stall. She walked over and picked it up. It wasn't new, but it certainly wasn't fifty years old, either.

"Is this what you want?" she asked, handing it to him.

He took it from her without any thanks or acknowledgment.

"I need more than a rake. I need another pair of hands. This place is too much for me to take care of."

Susan looked at the white-haired man, who, she knew without any doubt, was Ben.

"I'll help you." The words seemed to fly out of her mouth.

The old man looked at her through narrowed eyes.

"I never had a girl help with the raking."

Susan's face flushed. "I can rake as well as anyone," she said, although the truth was that she had never raked before.

Ben hesitated, then grudgingly handed the rake back to her.

"We'll see how you do. You can start down by the gate and go all along the fence. I'll be working up by the house."

For the rest of the morning and into the early afternoon, Susan raked. Every now and then she stepped back to admire the mounds of leaves that bordered the fence like newly sprouted bushes. When she got hungry, she went inside for lunch, stopping first to see Aunt Elizabeth, who was writing letters in the library.

"You won't need to get a helper for Ben," Susan announced proudly. "I've been raking for him all morning."

The old lady raised her eyebrows. "Are you sure that's what you want to be doing on your holiday?"

"I don't mind. It's sort of fun. I'm going back out after lunch."

Susan raked all through the afternoon. When it began to grow dark, she looked around for Ben, but he was nowhere to be seen.

She leaned the rake against the side of the stable and turned to go back to the house.

Just then, the stable door swung open and out hobbled Alex on his crutches.

"Well now, who are you and what are you doing snooping around here?"

He was smiling, but even in the half-light Susan could tell that his eyes were cold.

She opened her mouth to speak. Nothing came out.

Alex limped closer to her.

"You're not another Jew-girl she's taken in, are you?"

For the first time in her life, Susan felt her Jewishness.

"I'm Susan," she stammered. "I'm here visiting for a week."

"Well, stay away from these stables, do you hear? Those are my horses, and no one else is allowed to ride them."

"I'm not interested in your horses. I don't even know how to ride."

Alex laughed, but his eyes remained cold.

"Make sure you keep it that way. We

wouldn't want you falling off and breaking your leg, would we?"

He laughed again and hobbled back inside the stables.

Susan stood frozen for a moment before she turned and ran toward Wimsley Hall.

CHAPTER
6

Susan excused herself from tea that afternoon, saying she wasn't feeling well. When Mrs. Spruce brought up a tray, she set it on the table by the bed and put her hand on Susan's forehead.

"You're all right," she said. "But you don't want to be working too hard, now. It's one thing to help someone out and another to wear yourself out."

She walked over to the door. "Call me if you need anything."

"Mrs. Spruce?"

"Yes? What is it?"

Susan didn't know what to say. She wanted

to tell someone about Alex, but she didn't know how. She knew she wouldn't be believed. She hardly believed it herself.

"Nothing, I guess."

Mrs. Spruce sighed, then closed the door gently behind her.

The wind began blowing again, as it had every night since Susan arrived, only this time the sound seemed to echo inside the house.

At first she tried to ignore it, but it persisted, even when the wind outside stopped. Then she realized that what she heard was not the wind at all but the sound of someone crying.

Hesitantly, she got out of bed and opened her door. She followed the sound to a room at the end of the hallway. By then, the crying had subsided to intermittent sobbing.

Susan stood at the closed door, wanting to knock yet afraid. Quickly, before she could change her mind, she raised her hand and knocked twice.

The sobbing stopped immediately, and after a moment a voice murmured, "Come in."

Susan turned the knob and slowly pushed the door open.

The room was a mirror image of hers, with the same type of bed, night table, and dresser, all set against opposite walls. Sitting on the bed, in a white flannel nightgown, was a girl with dark braids.

Susan immediately recognized her from the photograph she had seen last night.

"Are you Hanni?" she asked.

The girl nodded. Next to her, on the night table, was a menorah, exactly like the one Aunt Elizabeth kept on the table in the library. It held four unlit candles.

"I am about to light the Hanukkah candles," Hanni said.

She struck a match and lit the shamash candle. Then she said the prayers.

"We praise You, Lord our God, for commanding us to kindle the Hanukkah lights.

"We praise You, Lord our God, for the help You have given the Jewish people long ago at this time of the year."

She handed the shamash candle to Susan. "You may light the others," she said.

Almost as if in a trance, Susan lit the remaining candles and replaced the shamash candle in its holder. She realized that the candles she had seen burning in the window the other night had been Hanni's.

Hanni carried the menorah to the window and placed it on the sill. When she turned back to Susan, tears streamed from her eyes.

"I am sorry for crying," she said. "I am thinking about other Hanukkahs, when I was home with my parents. They sent me here to be safe, but I do not feel safe being away from them."

Susan stared at her. "Where did you come from?" she asked. Although she knew from Hanni's accent that she was foreign, her question wasn't referring to a particular place. It was more a statement of wonder.

But Hanni replied matter-of-factly, through her tears, "I am from Vienna. At least that is where I lived before the war, before Hitler came to power, before Kristallnacht."

"Kristall what?"

"Kristallnacht. The Night of Broken Glass," Hanni said. "That was the night the Nazis burned Jewish synagogues and businesses. They broke all the windows of my father's clothing store and stole his merchandise. There had been restrictions against the Jews before Kristallnacht, but afterward it was much worse. I was not allowed to attend school anymore and my Gentile friends were forbidden to speak to me." Hanni started to cry again. "My parents sent me to London. They said they would try to follow me soon, but it has been almost two years now."

"How did you get here?" Susan asked. This time she meant it literally.

"I was staying with a family in London. When the Blitz—the bombing—began, I was put on a train with hundreds of other children, and after many stops I was told to get off at this village. Elizabeth was at the station, and she took me and brought me here. I am very grateful to her. She has been very kind and has tried to help me contact my parents, but so far we have not been able to find them. I am afraid something has happened to them. I am afraid I will never see them again."

She wiped her eyes with a handkerchief. "I am also afraid of Elizabeth's stepson."

"Do you mean Alex?" Susan asked, wide-eyed.

Hanni nodded. "He hates me just because I am Jewish."

"I am Jewish, too," Susan said. For the second time that day, she was acutely aware of being Jewish.

"Why are *you* here?" Hanni asked.

For a moment, Susan was taken aback. She could barely remember her own circumstances after listening to Hanni's story. When she spoke, it was in simple, disjointed sentences.

"I am visiting Elizabeth. I am a relative of hers. My name is Susan. My father—"

At that moment, the sound of a baby's crying interrupted her.

"That is just little Malcolm," Hanni said. "He is Elizabeth's nephew. Are you related to him?"

Susan sat down on the bed next to Hanni, stunned with the realization that the crying baby was her own father!

"Yes, I guess I am," she said.

"You look like you have seen a ghost," Hanni said.

Susan reached out and touched Hanni's hand. It seemed real enough, yet how could it be? She wasn't sure of anything anymore.

"So many strange things have been happening since I came here," she said.

"Like what?"

"Like seeing Alex and Jamie and the horses in the stables."

"What is strange about that?" Hanni asked. "To me, the only strange thing is why Alex hates me so much. He has threatened to hurt me if I ride his horses."

"He said that to me, too. It doesn't matter. I don't know how to ride anyway."

"I do," Hanni said. "I used to ride horses in the countryside at home. I miss it very much. I think I would not be as homesick if I could ride again."

"Have you asked Elizabeth?"

"I do not wish to trouble her. She is busy with the baby and the army hospital in the village. I am busy, too, helping with the baby.

That is good because then I do not think about my parents, or about Alex. But I would like to ride—if only just once."

She started to cry again, and Susan took her hand, surprised at the tears in her own eyes.

Hanni stopped crying. "Are you homesick, too?" she asked.

Susan looked at Hanni for a long time before she answered.

"Yes," she finally said. "I guess I am."

CHAPTER

7

Susan woke up to the sound of rain beating on the window. It made her think of Hanni's tears.

She and Hanni had stayed up late the night before, talking, crying, and, after a while, even laughing. By the time Susan went back to her room, she felt as if she and Hanni were old friends.

As she lay in bed thinking about Hanni and listening to the rain, an idea popped into her head.

She would ask Jamie to take Hanni riding on the moor. He could get the horses ready, and she would bring Hanni to the stables at what-

ever time they set—a time when Alex wouldn't
be around.

Susan pictured Hanni smiling when she
heard the plan. The more Susan thought about
it, the more excited she became. She couldn't
wait to tell her friend.

She threw off the covers and, without even
putting on her slippers, ran barefoot down the
hall to Hanni's room. She knocked on the door
softly in case Hanni was still sleeping.

"Hanni, it's me. Are you awake?"

She waited a moment. Then she pushed the
door open and walked into the room.

It was cold and empty, with the musty smell
of a long-vacated place. There were no sheets
or covers on the bed, no Hanukkah menorah—and no Hanni.

Susan sat down on the bare mattress. With a
mixture of disappointment and wonder, she
realized that the only time she had ever seen
Jamie, Alex, and then Hanni was at dusk or at
night, never during the day.

But as she looked around the empty room,
she began to doubt that she had really talked to
Hanni last night. It had seemed so real at the

time, yet how could it be? Hanni was from the past, just the way Alex and Jamie were. They didn't exist in the light of day.

A shiver ran through her. There were only two explanations for what was happening.

Are Hanni and the others ghosts? she asked herself. Or am I going crazy?

When she went down to breakfast, she tried to be casual but, as usual, blurted out her question.

"Do you believe in ghosts?" she asked her great-aunt as she sat down at the table.

She held her breath, expecting that Aunt Elizabeth might laugh or, at the very least, stare at her, but the old woman only pursed her lips and thoughtfully considered her answer.

"It depends on what you mean by ghosts," she said. "I don't believe in see-through creatures that run around in white sheets. But I do think that sometimes, under special circumstances, we can get a glimpse of what happened a long time ago."

"Have you ever seen anyone . . . from a long time ago?" Susan asked.

"Well, I thought I did, once or twice."

"Me, too. I mean, I thought I did."

Susan blushed at her revelation and concentrated more than usual on spreading the jam on her toast.

Aunt Elizabeth nodded, as if she had been expecting Susan to say that.

"Whatever it is, you need to trust what you saw. It doesn't matter whether it makes sense or not, or whether others believe you or not. What matters is what's true for you."

Susan felt relieved. If Aunt Elizabeth didn't think she was crazy, maybe she wasn't.

She finished breakfast without asking any more questions, and when Aunt Elizabeth suggested going into the village, Susan readily accepted.

They drove there in Aunt Elizabeth's minivan. All the while, Susan kept picturing her great-aunt riding a horse along that same country road.

Susan spent most of the day shopping for souvenirs to bring home, while Aunt Elizabeth tended to her errands. Later they met for lunch in the local pub. By the time they returned to Wimsley Hall, the rain had stopped, although the sky was still cloudy and beginning to grow dark.

All day, Susan had been thinking about her plan to help Hanni go horseback riding. Now that it was dusk, she decided to find Jamie and make the arrangements with him.

"I'll take a quick walk-about," she announced as she got out of the car. "I need to stretch my legs."

"Don't be too long," Aunt Elizabeth said. "Mrs. Spruce will have tea waiting."

Susan headed toward the stables, praying she wouldn't have to go inside to look for Jamie. She didn't want to risk running into Alex again.

With a sigh of relief, she saw Jamie in the distance, coming off the moor, leading a horse by the reins. She walked over to the courtyard and waited for him.

"I forgot to introduce myself the other day," she said as he approached. She spoke loudly, over the clip-clop of the horse's hooves on the gravel. "I'm Susan."

Jamie nodded but kept on walking the horse past her toward the stables.

"I wanted to ask you something," she called after him.

"I got to be bringing in the horse."

"I just wanted to ask you a favor."

He stopped and waited.

"I wanted to know if you could take Hanni riding on the moor with you."

He stared at her, as if she had asked him to take someone to the moon.

"Alex has given orders that no one's to ride the horses. I only take them out to exercise them."

"But she just wants to ride once, for a little while. She would be helping you exercise them. He probably wouldn't even find out."

Jamie kept looking at Susan in silence, considering the idea. A slow smile crossed his face.

"It would be a laugh on him, now, wouldn't it? It would almost be worth getting fired over."

"Elizabeth wouldn't fire you," Susan said.

"If he keeps telling her lies about me, she might."

"I'll tell her the truth."

He was silent again for a moment. Then he

said, "Bring her to the stables about this time tomorrow. We'll ride for half an hour before it gets too dark."

At tea, Susan offered to light the Hanukkah candles. After she lit the shamash candle, she slowly repeated the prayers she had heard Hanni say, word for word.

"Where did you learn that?" Aunt Elizabeth asked, astonished.

"I remembered it," Susan said. "From a long time ago," she added.

The girl could barely sit through the rest of tea. She thought her great-aunt's stories about the army hospital would go on forever.

As soon as she thought it reasonably polite, she excused herself and went upstairs. She went straight to Hanni's room and knocked on the door.

"Come in," a soft voice said.

Susan walked in and found Hanni placing the already lit menorah on the windowsill.

"I waited for you, but you did not come."

"It's all right," Susan said. "I have exciting news."

She proceeded to tell Hanni about her plan and her conversation with Jamie.

"But what if Alex sees me?" Hanni asked, alarm in her eyes.

"Don't worry. I'll look out for him and distract him if I have to."

Hanni still looked worried, but she finally agreed.

"All right, but perhaps we should tell Elizabeth."

"I don't think so." Susan wasn't used to sharing secrets with adults. Besides, her plan was already in place; everything was set.

"The fewer people we tell, the better," she said. "I'll come for you right at sunset tomorrow."

"Can you come earlier?" Hanni asked.

Susan smiled. "It wouldn't work any earlier." She gave Hanni a hug. "I'll see you tomorrow at sunset."

CHAPTER

8

The next day seemed to drag on endlessly for Susan, although she tried to keep herself busy. She and Aunt Elizabeth walked on the moor before breakfast. Then she raked until lunch, and in the afternoon they went into the village.

The sky had threatened rain all day, but it wasn't until they were driving back to Wimsley Hall that it actually started to shower.

"We're lucky the rain's held off until now," Aunt Elizabeth said, pulling into the driveway.

Susan didn't think it was so lucky. The rain made her uneasy. What if it spoiled her plan?

She wanted to find Jamie and make sure

everything was still set, but she decided to go inside and get Hanni ready first.

After telling Aunt Elizabeth she needed to rest before tea, she went upstairs to Hanni's room and knocked on the door.

"Hanni, it's me—Susan. Let me in."

No one answered.

She pushed the door open. The room was just as it had been the other morning—completely deserted.

It must be too early, she thought. It must not be dusk yet. It must have only seemed that way because of the rain.

She went to her own room and stood by the window watching the rain coming down harder now. As she stood there, worrisome thoughts raced through her mind.

What if the whole thing had to be called off because of the rain? What if Hanni changed her mind? What if Alex found out and spoiled everything?

Suddenly, she realized it was long past sunset. She hurried back to Hanni's room.

The door was half-open. Even without going in, though, she could see that the room was still deserted.

The only thing she could think of was that Hanni hadn't waited for her and had already gone out to meet Jamie.

Susan ran down the stairs and grabbed an umbrella from the stand by the door. With rain beating down on it, she ran to the stables, lifted the rusty latch and pulled the door open.

She was afraid of finding Alex, but she was even more afraid of what she found instead.

Nothing. No horses, no Hanni, no Jamie; not even Alex.

Where has everyone gone? she asked herself. Why have they all disappeared? Did the rain wash them away?

"Where are you?" she shouted at the empty stables. "Where are you?"

But no one answered.

CHAPTER

9

It rained steadily for the next two days and nights. Each evening at sunset, Susan went to Hanni's room and then to the stables. But there was no trace of Hanni, Jamie, Alex, or the horses.

Despite her intense disappointment, Susan kept herself busy. Before breakfast that first rainy morning, she and Aunt Elizabeth took a long walk on the moor.

"We have to walk in the rain or we can't do any walking at all now, can we?" her great-aunt said as they set off across the moor carrying umbrellas. They wore slickers and

Wellies, the tall green boots that kept their feet dry.

Later that day, Susan helped Aunt Elizabeth arrange the books in the library in neat alphabetical rows. It wasn't as boring a task as she had thought it might be. In fact, she rather enjoyed it. She felt the same satisfaction that she did raking leaves for Ben.

Afterward she helped Mrs. Spruce with her cooking. They made potato pancakes, which the housekeeper said was an Irish dish as well as a traditional Hanukkah food.

Cooking was the most fun of all for Susan. She had never done any before and felt proud at tea when her great-aunt commented on how good the potato pancakes tasted.

The next morning, Aunt Elizabeth had an early errand, and Susan went out on the moor alone. She remembered all the landmarks her great-aunt had shown her to keep her on the right path. With some surprise, she realized she would miss the heather and the rest of the scrubby landscape that had become so familiar to her.

She tried not to think about Hanni or Jamie and didn't speak of them to anyone. But at tea on the seventh night of Hanukkah, after she lit the candles, she blurted out a question that had been bothering her ever since she first saw Hanni.

"Did Hanni ever find her parents?" Susan asked her great-aunt.

"I don't know," Aunt Elizabeth said. "They never came here for her, and we tried unsuccessfully to contact them. It's likely they were killed by the Nazis, although I suppose it's possible she was reunited with them in Israel. She went there after the war, but I lost touch with her."

Suddenly, Susan burst into tears.

"I've lost touch with her, too," she sobbed. "I don't know where she's gone. She's just disappeared."

Aunt Elizabeth looked at Susan with a puzzled frown. She was about to say something but instead put her arm around her great-niece and just held her gently while the girl cried.

"I believe that nothing is ever really lost,"

the old woman finally said. "It's always somewhere. Sometimes, when things don't seem to
be going the way we want them to, it may not
be the right time for them yet. But it will be,
and we just have to keep on going till then.
Remember the heather? It just keeps on going and going and going, and eventually it
blooms."

Susan took the tissue her great-aunt handed
her and blew her nose. She felt comforted by
Aunt Elizabeth's words, even though she didn't
really understand them.

When she was by herself, though, lying in
bed, listening to the wind and the rain, her
sadness returned.

This time it wasn't about losing Hanni or
having her plan spoiled. It was a deeper loss,
one she thought she had put behind her a long
time ago.

But in fact, having been held and comforted
by her great-aunt had brought back the mem-
ory of being taken care of by her mother. She
felt like a little girl again and realized how
much she had missed her mother, how much

she still missed her. She had lied to herself all these years, pretending she didn't need her mother—or anyone else for that matter. Now she was facing the truth.

The tears frozen inside her for so long were melting, washing away the lie. And the melting tears seemed endless, like the rain that beat on the window.

CHAPTER

10

On the morning of the last night of Hanukkah, on the day before Susan was to leave Wimsley Hall, she woke up and realized that something had changed.

The rain had ended.

She looked out the window and saw the sun burning through high clouds. The moor was sparkling in the sunlight. Its still-wet heather blossomed with millions of tiny rainbows.

Something in Susan had changed, too. The torrent of tears she had cried the night before seemed to have created a space inside her. It wasn't a lonely space. It was more like the anticipation of something new, something so new she couldn't quite name it.

In fact, everything seemed new to her, even the activities that had become familiar over the past week—walking on the moor before breakfast with her great-aunt, going into the village on a few errands, helping Mrs. Spruce with her cooking, and then, later in the afternoon, raking.

"Are you sure you want to be doing that on your last full day here?" Aunt Elizabeth asked as Susan was heading outside.

"I haven't been able to help Ben these past few days because of the rain. I don't want him to think I've forgotten."

Susan did want to help the old gardener, but she also wanted to be outdoors alone for a little while. As she raked, she thought through all the events that had taken place since that first evening when she saw Jamie raking. So many things had happened. So much had changed.

Suddenly, the clip-clop of horses' hooves broke into her thoughts. She spun around, and there behind her was Jamie, leading two saddled horses out of the stables.

"I got them ready," he said. "Where is she?"

Struck by his sudden appearance, Susan was silent for a moment. She wanted to ask him where he had been the last few days but realized that probably time hadn't passed in the same way for him that it had for her.

"I'll go get her," she said, but as Susan started running toward the house, Hanni appeared in the courtyard.

"Stay here and keep an eye out for Alex," Jamie instructed Susan as he led the horses toward Hanni. "We'll be back in half a while."

Susan watched as they mounted the horses and rode onto the moor. Her plan had worked! Even if Alex showed up right now, at least Hanni's wish had come true.

As she was congratulating herself, a black car pulled into the driveway, stopping just past the front gate.

Susan had never seen it before and held her breath while she waited for someone to get out.

Seconds passed, but no one emerged from the car. Becoming more and more frightened, she started to run toward the stables but tripped over the rake.

She picked herself up, her heart pounding, and ran behind the building. From there, looking around the corner, she could see a man and a woman walking up the driveway. They were both wearing suits and hats that looked like they had once been stylish but now were well worn. They kept stopping and looking about, as if they weren't sure which way to go.

At least they didn't appear to be threatening.

Susan was just about to come out of her hiding place when she heard the rustling of leaves nearby. Alex hobbled out of the woods on his crutches. "Who might you be looking for?" he shouted down the driveway at the couple.

The man stepped forward. "We were told our daughter is staying here," he said with a German accent.

"And who would that be?"

"Her name is Hanni."

"Oh yes," Alex said, nodding his head in recognition. "Hanni."

Susan couldn't see his face, but she knew he was smiling and that, in spite of his smile, his eyes were cold.

"She was here," Alex continued, "but she's not anymore."

The man looked alarmed. "Where has she gone?"

Alex spoke slowly and deliberately.

"She went to London. She left a few weeks ago. She said she'd tell us where she was, but we haven't heard from her yet."

The woman was clutching the man's arm, excitedly asking him questions in German. He turned to her and answered in German, as reassuringly as he could. Then he handed Alex a piece of paper.

"We will be going back to London then. If she contacts you, give her this number, please."

Alex took the piece of paper and put it in his pocket. "I'll do that," he said.

Susan's heart was beating so loudly, she was certain that both Alex and Hanni's parents could hear it. Frozen with fear, she watched the couple turn and walk slowly down the driveway to the waiting car at the gate. She watched the man help the woman into the car. She watched him start to get in after her.

Then she burst out of her hiding place.

"Wait!" she shouted, running down the driveway past Alex. "He's lying! Hanni really is here."

Alex hobbled after Susan, enraged.

"Don't believe her," he shouted to Hanni's parents, who were getting back out of the car again. "She's a liar. An interfering liar." He held out a crutch threateningly toward Susan.

At that moment, Jamie and Hanni were returning from the moor. They were laughing and in high spirits as they trotted over the gravel courtyard, heading toward the stables.

When they heard the commotion at the gate, they reined in their horses and stopped.

Jamie jumped off his horse and held both pairs of reins while Hanni, already dismounted, was running down the driveway crying, "Mama! Papa!"

As Hanni and her parents embraced, Susan grabbed Alex's crutch and jerked it toward her, making Alex fall to the ground.

CHAPTER

11

"We are so very grateful for what you did," Hanni said to Susan.

Susan blushed. She was sitting in the library, next to the fireplace, across from Hanni and her parents.

"Did you see how Alex scrambled away when Jamie came after him?" Susan asked, trying to take some of the attention away from herself.

"Yes, but it was you who stood up to his lie," Hanni said. "If you hadn't, my parents would have driven away without finding me, and we would be lighting the candles alone," Hanni said.

The menorah was on the tea table with nine unlit candles in its holders.

"I hope Elizabeth comes back soon, so we can light the candles," Susan said, still trying to change the subject.

Just then, as if on cue, Elizabeth entered the room, carrying a baby in her arms.

She was not the old woman Susan knew but the young woman she had seen in the photograph. In fact, both Elizabeth and the baby were wearing the same clothes they had on in the photograph.

With a gasp, Susan realized that the chubby baby in Elizabeth's arms was her own father! Her heart was beating faster than when she had run down the driveway to stop Hanni's parents from leaving.

"I'm sorry to have kept you waiting," Elizabeth said, "but little Malcolm was being fussy."

She turned to Susan. "Would you like to hold him?"

Susan took the baby and looked into his eyes, the same hazel eyes her father had, except the baby's eyes were wet with tears.

She had never thought about how sad and

lonely it must have been for him, too, to be separated from his parents at such an early age. She hugged the baby, and tears of forgiveness toward her grown-up father rolled down her cheeks.

"You light the candles tonight, Susan," Hanni said.

Susan handed the baby back to Elizabeth and lit the shamash candle.

Then Hanni's father led everyone in saying the blessings, first in Hebrew and then in English. When they finished, he said, "There is another prayer, one we usually say on the first night of Hanukkah, but I think it is fitting to say it tonight."

His voice trembled with emotion as he recited it. "We praise You, Lord our God, for keeping us alive and well so that we may enjoy this holiday."

"Amen," Elizabeth said.

"Amen," they all repeated, and Susan lit the remaining eight candles.

For a few moments, they all watched the candle flames dancing. Their glow seemed to light up the whole room.

At last, Hanni broke the silence.

"When I was little," she said, "after we lit the Hanukkah candles, we would play a game with a tiny top called a dreidel. You would spin the dreidel, and depending on which side it landed on, you would either win or lose a candy or keep what you had."

"It had letters on each of its sides," her father went on to explain. "The letters spelled out a sentence in Hebrew: 'A great miracle happened here.'

"You see, a long time ago, against great odds, the Jewish people won a victory over a powerful enemy. To give thanks for the victory, a lamp in the Temple was lit. There was only enough oil for the lamp to burn one day, but the lamp burned for eight days—truly a miracle. That is why we celebrate Hanukkah."

"Well, I think a great miracle happened here tonight," Elizabeth said, looking at Susan and making her blush again. "Perhaps more than one miracle," she added.

Hanni's father had been translating everything into German for his wife. Now he leaned over to hear what she was saying.

"My wife says that Hanukkah is a time of many miracles. It is a time of the deepest darkness, and out of that deep darkness comes the brightest light."

"Yes, that's true," Elizabeth agreed. "Whenever we face our own darkness—our own deep fear and deep sadness—we create a miracle of healing."

Hanni's father reached into his pocket for a handkerchief to blow his nose.

"Here is yet another miracle," he said, bringing out a tiny flat-sided top. "I did not even know it was here."

"Oh, Papa, my dreidel," Hanni cried with delight.

She showed everyone how to play with the dreidel, and they played, and talked, and drank tea, and ate potato pancakes, until late into the night.

CHAPTER

12

Susan knew when she woke up the next morning that Hanni and her parents, and Jamie and Alex, and the young Elizabeth, and baby Malcolm would all be gone.

Today she would be leaving, too. She tried not to think about that as she and Aunt Elizabeth set out for a walk on the moor before breakfast. But when they climbed the hill that overlooked the moor on one side and the valley on the other, she turned to her great-aunt.

"You were right last week when you said I was homesick. I am homesick. Right now, I'm homesick for you and the moor and

Wimsley Hall and everyone I met here—even Alex."

She started to cry and didn't see Aunt Elizabeth's eyebrows raised in surprise.

"Alex?"

Susan nodded and, in between her tears, proceeded to tell her great-aunt exactly what had happened, from the day she arrived all the way up through the previous night.

"Well, it's quite wonderful, isn't it?" Aunt Elizabeth said after Susan had finished. "It really is a miracle after all."

"But did it happen? Did I really stop Alex? You once told me that Hanni left here and probably never did meet up with her parents."

"Well, we don't know how things turned out, do we?" Aunt Elizabeth said. "We don't know whether what you did more than fifty years later changed things or not. I suspect that somehow it did."

She put her arm around Susan. "At least you've changed."

"I know," Susan sniffed. "I can't believe it, but I actually feel sorry for Alex!"

"Well, Alex was homesick, too. He missed his parents and never forgave them for not being there for him. Of course, he took his pain out on others, which you rightly stood up to."

"What happened to him?" Susan asked.

"Eventually his leg healed, and he enlisted in the army." She paused for a moment. "He was killed in battle soon after."

Tears welled up again in Susan's eyes. "What about Jamie?" she said.

"Didn't you guess?"

The girl shook her head.

"Jamie is short for Benjamin."

"You mean Ben is Jamie?"

Aunt Elizabeth nodded. "As he got older, he thought Ben suited him better."

"They're all gone—or grown old," Susan cried. "Nothing stays the same."

"I'm afraid you're right," Aunt Elizabeth said. "The only thing we can be sure of is that everything changes."

They walked back to Wimsley Hall in silence, not needing to say anything else.

After breakfast, Aunt Elizabeth came up to Susan's room to help her pack.

"I hope you have room for this," she said. She handed her the small brass menorah. "I think Hanni would want you to have it."

Susan took the menorah from the old woman, as carefully as she had taken baby Malcolm the night before, and held it to her heart.

"I feel like I'm not leaving any of you behind after all," she said.

"Well, I hope you'll miss us enough to want to come back next year," Aunt Elizabeth said. "Perhaps you can persuade your father to come along, too."

"I hope so," Susan said.

She wrapped the menorah in a T-shirt and put it in her knapsack. "It's sad to leave, though."

"Saying good-bye always is," Aunt Elizabeth said. "But out of endings come beginnings."

"You mean, the way out of darkness comes light?" Susan asked.

Aunt Elizabeth smiled. "Where did you hear that?"

"Right here, in the library at Wimsley Hall," Susan said. "Only I'm not sure if it was last night or fifty years ago."

"Maybe it was both," Aunt Elizabeth said. "After all, anything can happen at Hanukkah. It's a time of miracles."